RAIN OF DYSTOPIA

JACLYN ANDREWS

authorHOUSE®

AuthorHouse™
1663 Liberty Drive
Bloomington, IN 47403
www.authorhouse.com
Phone: 1 (800) 839-8640

Cover art by Robert A. Gaines

Published by AuthorHouse 02/15/2018

ISBN: 978-1-5462-2948-3 (sc)
ISBN: 978-1-5462-2947-6 (e)

Print information available on the last page.

This book is printed on acid-free paper.

Introduction

When I decided to write something, the first thing I said was. "What the hell am I going to about." So, I thought of what I was really into, and well I love Science Fiction and Sword and Sorcery and decided to create something with those topics and if you are wondering what I created with them, well, you're reading it as I speak. It began as a short story called the Dystopian Girl. it was about twelve pages long and took about thirteen hours to finish. This had been the first short story I had written since I dropped out of high school. I sent it to a good friend of mine to check it out, and he absolutely loved it. So, I decided to blow it up into a novel. This book is very important to me because it is my first novel and my friends and family encouraged me to live my dream as a writer. This book contains a lot emotion and friendship which is something I have always felt is very important in life, because the road gets dark and the sky gets cloudy but if that friend is right by your side you don't ever have to worry about going through it alone. I hope you enjoy this book as much as I did writing it, and remember dreams are not impossible to reach, just as long as you don't give up on yourself.

Jaclyn Andrews
2/6/18

This book is dedicated in the loving memory of Robert D. Gaines for being a great father and for teaching me, my brother, and my two little sisters so many wonderful things in life, and how to always look on the bright side. You had the biggest heart in the world. I love you Pop.

Rain, would often stare into the stars at night, hoping she could touch one. She has always been very curious about them, what magic could be held in them. She would also think about the stories Madame Oakeress would tell her of the past life and how the world fell into a dystopian wasteland. Growing up around Madame Oakeress she learned a lot about spiritual magic, mythical symbols, and what the power of the earth could hold. Madame Oakeress was one of the leaders in the Last Forests, she was the healer and the fortune teller. Many of the women in the Last Forests come to visit Madame Oakeress with questions of the future and what it might hold, but Rain always kept away from the future frightened of what it might tell her.

One night while Rain was laying on the roof of her hut, she saw a shape in the stars, a triangle with a K in it. The stars can tell many stories and symbolize different meanings. She thought to herself that she would tell Madame Oakeress about it in the morning after target practice with her friend Jillian. Rain carefully got off the roof making sure not to disturb her mother while she slept. Once Rain made it inside her hut she poured herself a glass of water and laid down in her bed. Her room was filled with stones and artifacts of the past such as, glasses, spoons, books, dolls, women's shoes, clocks, and many other things. She loved to collect antiques, they were so fascinating. When she fell asleep that night she dreamt she was wandering through the forest, but the forest was somehow empty, and lifeless.

she walked deeper into the forest, but she started feel cold and as if she was being watched. She started to run and then herd something from behind chasing her and growling loud. She ran as fast as she could, then she pulled out a stone dagger she keeps in her bag and turned around. At first all she could see was a Shadow, then a big mouth full of sharp silver teeth opened, and she awoke.

That morning Rain got out of bed still shaking from the nightmare she had. She got dressed, grabbed her wooden spear, and stone dagger and walked out of her room. Her mother asked her if she wanted any breakfast? Rain grabbed a piece of bread and headed out the door. Rain was on her way to meet up with Jillian but first she had to stop and pick up an empty scroll and a coal stick, so she can draw out the image she saw in the stars the night before, to show Madame Oakeress. She Saw Carol the shop owner and requested the items. "Are you ready for the festival tonight?" asked carol. "Of course, Carol I just need to practice my aim, and I'll be ready." Rain replied with a smile. "Oh, the big spear contest is my favorite part of the festival. I'll be there to cheer you on, Rain." Carol said as Rain smiled and walked away. The festival was an important event for the Last Forests, it only happens once a year. the festival brings the men and women villages together for one night. It all started when the world was dying the men and women escaped to the only surviving forest they could find. It's now known as The Last Forests for being so big. The men and women spent years building a great wall surrounding the inner part of the forest to hide the villages from any intruders. During its time of construction, the men and women grew to hate each other for reasons of sexism and equal rights to leadership. The men and women agreed to live in separate villages, but to also help each other out with supplies and crops. When the festival comes around men and women get together for games, contests, stories, hot food, jewelry, clothes, intimacy, and to witness the Great Divide. The Great divide is when the children born from the last festival, are put in their proper villages. If the child was born male it goes with the male villagers, and if it is female it goes with female villagers.

Rain arrived at Jillian's hut, and Jillian was walking out the door with her spear in hand. Jillian was wearing a forest green skirt around her waist and a forest green cloth like shirt. Jillian's clothes were much like Rains only, Rain's clothes were faded white, and Jillian's hair was red and tied in a knot with a vine, while Rain's hair was black, and she always kept her hair down. Rain and Jillian walked to the training area, just down the path from Jillian's hut, when they got there the area was completely empty. "who goes first?" Jillian asked. "Be my guest." Rain replied. Jillian lifted her spear and launched it at the target made of hay, ten yards away from them. she hit the highest ring, then Rain threw hers hitting the target dead center. "I don't think you even need to practice, Rain." said Jillian while she pulled both spears from the target. "Yeah, I do, I'm a decent shot but I get easily distracted. don't worry about me keep practicing." Rain told Jillian while concerned about the contest. The festival was tonight, so Rain needed to make sure she was perfectly ready for what's to come. "Don't be so serious, Rain. It's not that big of a deal." Jillian said looking at rain. "To me it is, I need to know that I can defend myself if ever the situation arises." Rain said as she looked at Jillian seriously for a moment, then smiled. "You are so dramatic." Jillian said shrugging off the tension.

They continued to practice, but all Rain could think about was the symbol she saw in the stars. What did it mean? Was it a sign? She knew if anyone could tell her, Madame Oakeress, would be the one to tell her what it is or what it means.

"Wow, for someone who doesn't like distractions, you really seem distracted." Jillian said.

"Shut up." Rain replied.

"What's the matter?" Jillian asked.

"Nothing, don't worry about it." Said Rain.

Rain threw her spear with all her might and hit the target in the center piercing a hole straight through. "There is something I need to talk to Madame Oakeress about. Let's call it a day." Rain told Jillian in a frustrated voice, while pulling out her spear. "Sure, I'll walk with you over there." Jillian replied calm but concerned.

As Rain and Jillian walked through the village to Madame Oakeress's hut, they saw many of the women at the market places, and came across Shelly the village tough girl, and her girlfriend Olive. Shelly has a very competitive spirit, she would always give the other girls a tough time. Olive was sweeter, but also very adventurous, and Olive never stayed doing one thing.

"I'm going to eat you alive at the spear competition, Rain." Shelly said with a grin while looking at Rain menacingly. "I plan on watching you fail miserably." Rain replied. Shelly tried to grab Rain, but before she could Olive pulled her back. "Wait until to tonight." Olive told Shelly as they walked away. Rain and Jillian continued to walk to Madame Oakeress's hut. "Don't worry about Shelly, she is just full of herself." Jillian said. "I'm not, she should be worried about me." Rain said as they both laughed.

When they arrived at Madame Oakeress's hut, Madame Oakeress was out back by a fire. Madame Oakeress had dark grey robes, and long grey hair that she kept tied up. Madame Oakeress was the oldest women in the village, and new more about the past than anyone else. Rain and Jillian walked up to Madame Oakeress But Waited for her, while she spoke to the spirits of the past within the flames of the burning fire. Madame Okeress spoke to the spirits only when she needed answers not even she could answer, but only she could provide the magic which could summon them. The spirits are the elders and the wisest of all knowledge, they can tell the past and future.

When Madame Oakeress finished, she looked at Rain and Jillian. "come, let us go inside." said Madame Oakeress. They all went in to her hut through the back entrance. Madame Oakeress's hut was full of many different artifacts and her walls were full of paintings. she had shelves full of old books and scrolls, many of them telling great histories of heroes and myths. She had sculptures of female warriors in mythology. Rain looked at everything in amazement, she had never been inside Madame Oakeress's hut before. Madame Oakeress never let anybody in before because she felt the women would steal her things.

"Do not touch anything!" Madame Oakeress said sternly, while Rain tried to grab a bracelet. "I am only letting you two in because the spirits said that this was meant to happen. Now Rain I know why you have come, although I need to see the drawing in which you about to show me. I need to see that what you are about to show me, is true." Madame Oakeress said in a worried voice.

Rain pulled out her scroll and coal stick from her bag and began to draw the image of the triangle with a K in it. Madame Oakeress, stared at it quietly with a sad expression. Her eyes began to water, as she turned her head away from Rain and Jillian. Madame Oakeress walked to the kitchen and poured herself a glass of water. "Rain, I must speak to the Spirits of the past. Come to me tonight after the festival and come alone. There is much to discuss, and much to prepare you for." said Madame Oakeress. "What are you talking about? What do I need to prepare for? What is going to happen?" Rain, felt enormous waves of anxiety. "Just go to the festival, while I speak to the spirits. I'll tell you everything afterwards." Madame Oakeress said. Rain, looked at her for a moment scared and concerned, then left with Jillian back to the market places. Madame Oakeress, lowered her head and started to cry.

"What do you think Madame Oakeress is going to tell you?" asked Jillian.

"I'm not sure, but I'm scared. I don't want to go back, but I have to." Rain replied.

"Rain, just know that no matter what happens, I will be there for you. always." Jillian said. Rain, started to remember when she had first met Jillian, when they were little. Jillian was being bullied by several young girls because she was overweight, but Rain had stepped in and stopped them from hurting her any further. Jillian hated Rain at first because she didn't trust her, but eventually she grew to love her like a sister.

When Rain and Jillian got to the market places, they got a couple of pieces of bread from the bakery and headed to their favorite spot. It was by a pond, just out of the market places. As they both sat down they started to think about what Madame Oakeress said, and what is going to happen at the festival.

"You think your mother will be there to see you at the spear competition, Rain?" Jillian asked. "No, she never comes. Mother doesn't approve of me learning things that can inflict violence. She says it's not going to help me, because we have no use for it here anymore. I still do it because it means something to me." Rain replied. Jillian always loved this about Rain. Jillian always knew that Rain had a strong heart, the heart of a warrior.

Rain gazed into the pond, she saw all kinds of fish, and frogs swimming by. She started to throw pieces of bread into the water. "Hey, Rain, you remember how Madame Oakeress always tells us about reincarnation?" Jillian asked. "yeah, why?" Rain replied. "Do you think they were once people?" Jillian asked while pointing at the fish in the pond. "It's possible, but you will never know 'til you die. one thing is for sure though." Rain said. "what is that?" asked Jillian. "you're going to be a fish, when you get reincarnated." Rain said. "shut up!" Jillian said as she slugged Rain in the shoulder. they both laughed as they got up. "c'mon, the sun is almost out, and we have to get to the festival, and we have to get there early, to play games before the contest." Rain said in excitement.

Rain tried to put the words Madame Oakeress said in the back of her mind and focus on the festival. Jillian Picked a flower from the ground and gave it to Rain. "For luck." said Jillian. Rain stared at the flower as they walked, then put it in her bag. Rain looked at Jillian and smiled. Jillian understood what Rain was feeling, even if Rain tried to play it off.

When they got back to the market places, they saw all the women in the village, heading to the center of The Last Forests. Everyone had bags, spears, torches, food and barrels of hooch. the horses were pulling wagons carrying all sorts of things for the festival.

Rian and Jillian saw tents and could smell the smoke of the log fires in the distance, as they walked through the trail that led to the festival. The fire light got brighter as they drew closer. They could see the men in the distance helping the women get things ready as festival began.

Once Rain and Jillian got there, music was playing, Kids were running around, food was cooking, and people everywhere were drinking hooch, which is a homemade drink that gives an inebriated feeling. Rain was happy to see that everyone was having a wonderful time. "Do you think we'll find a mate tonight, Rain?" Jillian asked as she chuckled. "Believe me sweetie, men may try to swing their best form of words at me, but my poor desperate heart, knows not to fall for a drunk jackass." Rain replied feeling both humorous and nervous. "You're no fun." Jillian said giggling at Rain's smart reply.

"Jillian if you find someone, have fun, but I need to focus on the spear contest. It's going to start soon." Rain said calmly. "What you need is a drink, besides you said we could play some games." Jillian said looking at her with a sad face. "Alright, but just a few." Rain said smiling.

Rain and Jillian played several games and drank some hooch to ease the nerves. "You two come here!" A man at one of the stands shouted at Rain and Jillian. "You two ever played Three's the charm?" The man said. "The drinking game?" Rain asked. "yeah." The man said. "We don't plan on swimming in hooch sir." Rain replied. "c'mon, c'mon. We'll play a short game. Just three rounds 'tis all I ask?" He begged. "Ok, but just me against you." Rain said in a daring tone. "Well, well. What a brave challenge, I accept." the man said flirtatiously. "you know how to play, there is three cups, two cups contain two dice, one cup contains three dice. pick the one with three you win otherwise you'll have to drink a whole glass of hooch each time you lose. We choose a cup at the same time all three rounds; your friend mixes the cups." The man explained. "So best two out of three?" Rain asked. "Yes." He replied.

The man pulled out the seven dice and all three cups. Jillian grabbed them and started mixing them. The man pulled out to big cups and filled them to the top. "That's too much." Rain said. "you should have told me your limit before we started, Sweetheart." The man replied laughing at her. Rain was feeling angry. Jillian finished mixing the cups and placed them at the center of the stand. Jillian looked at Rain and winked at her.

"Let the game begin." The man said. They both grabbed a cup. The man looked at rain and began to count. "One. Two. Three." They both pulled them up. The man, had two dice. Rain, had three. "Drink up." Rain said. "Lucky shot." The man said unsatisfied, as he began to drink his glass. Jillian mixed the cups again. The man and Rain both grabbed a cup. "one. two. three." The man counted. They both lifted the cups. Rain had three. The man had two. "Third round you will drink, or you'll never forget my face, WENCH!" The man shouted. he slammed his glass after he drank it. The man began to get dizzy. Jillian, mixed the cups again. Rain, started to feel uncomfortable. "One! Two! Three!" The man shouted. They both grabbed a cup. The man looked at Rain and grinned viciously. They both lifted the cups. The man, had two dice. Rain, had three. The man knocked over the third cup and saw three dice. "Cheaters!!!" he shouted. The man pulled out a stone dagger and tried to stab Rain but missed. Rain threw her glass of hooch at him, and Jillian hit him on the head with her spear, using it like a club to knock him out.

The man fell to the ground, knocked out cold. Rain placed her glass in his hand. Rain, and Jillian then walked casually to the contest area. "I told you I have your back." Jillian said excitedly. "Why did you cheat for me?" Rain asked. "Because, that guy tries to get women drunk every year, so he can get them to mate with him. So, I decided to give you the upper hand. I brought dice with me in case we ran into him." Jillian replied. "What if he had grabbed one of the cups with three dice, the same time I did?" asked, Rain. "Then it would have ended a lot sooner." Jillian, replied. "Wow. Thanks." said Rain as they both laughed and walked to the contest area of the festival.

The spear contest was about to begin as soon as they got there. Both villages, would gather to see it. The spear contest, consists of four men, and four women. Each person had to hit three targets, and who ever makes first place, by hitting two or more targets in the center is dubbed the strongest warrior of this year's festival.

Rain and Jillian were getting ready, when Rain looked, and saw shelly walking up to them. "Hey, Rain." Shelly said, staring at Rain as she picked up her spear. "What do you want, Shelly?" Rain asked. "I'm not here to pick a fight with you. I just wanted to say that I'm sorry for how I acted earlier, and I wish you the best of luck." Replied Shelly. Rain looked at her for a second, seeing the sadness in her eyes and hearing the truth in her voice. Rain got up and shook her hand. "Good luck." Rain said.

The contest area was a big field, with two stages along the sides. One for the women, and one for the men. There were three big targets made of hay in the center. At the end of the field was a giant stage where the council of the villages sat. The entire council was there except one, Madame Oakeress. The only other female councilor was, Davina the councilor of new life. she would speak for the great divide and tell us the origin of The Last Forests. The male councilors were, Jerice the councilor of law, and Ashton the councilor of education and leadership. Madame Oakeress was the councilor of wisdom and magic.

Rain, Jillian, Shelly, and Olive, were the female contestants this year. Liam, Garret, Jonna, and Jackson, were the male contestants. They all got in line as Ashton got up to say a few words to everyone. "To everyone here tonight. these eight warriors shall give their best in this great challenge. They have trained all year round to Prove that they have what it takes to fight if ever given situation. Now please give them the chance to show you their skills, and abilities. You men and women have my blessings. Let the games begin!" Ashton sat back down as the audience clapped.

Women went first, Shelly walked up to the throwing area, there stood another woman with a bag of spears "Don't forget to mark your spear." the woman said. Shelly tied a vine on her spear, then launched it at the left target, hitting it on the outer rim. She grabbed a spear from the woman and launched it at the middle target hitting it in the center. She grabbed one more spear from the woman and launched it at the right target hitting the second to the last outer rim. Shelly lowered her head as the audience clapped. Jillian was next, she tied a beige ribbon on her spear, and launched it at the left target hitting the center of it. She threw her second spear at the middle target hitting the last outer rim. She threw her third spear at the right target hitting it in the center. So far Jillian was in the lead. As Olive went up, Jillian walked up to Rain. "Hey, don't get nervous. you're going to do great." Said Jillian. "I'm not that nervous, I just want to leave after this and head to Madame Oakeress's hut. I need to figure out what she needs to tell me." Rain said worried. Jillian looked at Rain and hugged her. "Don't worry about it. Just be strong." Rain smiled. It was Rain's turn, she tied a ribbon on her spear. She threw it at the first target hitting it in the center. She threw her second spear at the next target hitting it in the center. She threw her third spear, but while she was in mid throw someone from the audience called out her name, causing her to lose her aim and miss the target entirely. Two women got the same score, Jillian and Rain. The men went next first was Garret, then Jonna, Jackson, and last was Liam. Jonna was the only man who hit more than one target in the center. So Jonna had to challenge Jillian and Rain. Jillian went first but was only able to hit two targets. Jonna went next and hit only one target. Rain hit two targets but before she threw her third spear, she heard that voice call her name again. She realized it wasn't from the crowd it was Madame Oakeress, speaking in her mind telling her to leave the festival. Rain shook her head and threw her third spear hitting the target dead center. "We have a champion!!" Ashton shouted.

Rain, fell on her knees, she felt scared. Jillian walked up and congratulated her. "Jillian, I have to go!" Rain shouted. "Can't I go with you?" asked Jillian "No, I have to go alone." Rain Replied. "I'll be here when you get back." Said Jillian.

Rain grabbed her spear and bag and went back to the village. When she got to Madame Oakeress's hut, Rain saw Madame Oakeress standing outside staring at the moonlight. Before Rain could speak, she thought of all the possibilities Madame Oakeress could tell her about the symbol in the stars, and why it worried her so much. Rain was frightened of what it could mean.

"Come here Rain, let's go to the River Willows." Madame Oakeress told her. Rain stayed paused for a moment, Looked at Madame Oakeress, then started to walk towards her. "Will you tell me what this is all about?" Rain asked. "When we get there, my dear. Now come. we must go." said Madame Oakeress. They walked to the River Willows in silence. Rain

9

was scared, she looked at Madame Oakeress, but Madame Oakeress just kept looking straight into the darkness in silence, until they got to the River Willows.

As soon as they got there, they made a small fire. Madame Oakeress threw a stone into the river While deep in thought, then turned to look at Rain. "Rain, remember when you were young, and I would bring you and Jillian here so you two could speak to the spirits? You two would always want to speak the spirits of the pets you two once had." Madame Oakeress said as she walked back to the fire. "I do remember, Madame Oakeress. You said we could truly speak to them only if they knew we truly loved them." Replied Rain. "I'm such a bad liar." Madame Oakeress said. "What is it, that you need to tell me, Madame Oakeress?" Rain asked "I knew this day would come. The day I told the truth about the world." Madame Oakeress said as she started to cry. "Tell me!" Rain demanded.

"Everyone believes this world died by a great nuclear blast, but that's not true. that's not true at all! We made all of you believe that, so we could protect all of you from what is truly out there. Me and the others who survived the destruction of the world, but they have all passed and I am the only remaining person who helped build the villages and that great wall within the Last Forests. Along time ago, there was a woman named Kenya. Kenya built a small business called Kenya corps. They made computers, and eventually they grew and started to move towards scientific research. Once Kenya started to make cures for all kinds of diseases, she realized her success, she quickly became corrupt, greedy, and hungry for power. She wanted to rule the world. Kenya started creating genetic mutations to keep governments from trying to bring her down. Super soldiers that couldn't be stopped. They were called Junaks, Huge beast like creatures that stood on all fours, and looked more animal than man. the only thing the Junaks had that looked even remotely human was their heads, but with long sharp teeth. The Junaks eventually broke out of containment, and slaughtered everyone in Kenya corps. When the Junaks broke out of the building nothing could stop them because no matter how many times you try to kill a Junak it's blood develops a new body out of the blood cells that come out of the Junak. Making it multiply, so every time it bleeds a new Junak was born and they grew within minutes. There were thousands of them and eventually billions of them. That is the truth, Rain. This was one hundred and forty-five years ago." Madame Oakeress started to cry. "How do you Know so much about this? How do you know more than a normal survivor would? What are you really hiding from me, and what does this have to do with the triangle in the stars?" Rain asked in a rage for she had been lied to all her life. Madame Oakeress looked at her. "The triangle with a K in it means Kenya corps. I was Kenya's personal assistant." Madame Oakeress said as she started to weep again. Madame Oakeress continued. "Rain, When I worked with Kenya, she trusted me, but I found out how she developed a way to kill the Junaks. Kenya built microchips that were implanted into their brains. the microchips are the computers that trigger the mutant blood cells to create a new body. because of this, the cell also must create a new microchip that functions like the older one. The microchip can release acid in to the body killing the Junak instantly. Kenya did this in case any Junaks tried to attack her. Rain I could have saved the world the night the Junaks broke out, but before I could, Kenya locked herself in the room where the self-destruct button for the Junaks is. Years later the spirits of the past told me that one day a girl will rise to save and rebuild this dying world we live in. When I spoke to the spirits about the symbol today, they informed me that the time has come, and it is you who must fulfil this destiny."

Rain shook her head and began to cry. "No! Not me. I can't. what am I supposed to do? I mean, I'm just. I don't want to do this." Rain sat down and continued to cry. "Rain, this is who you are. This what you were meant to do." Madame Oakeress said. "I'm just scared. Okay. What do I got to do?" Rain asked sobbing.

"You must go to the edge of the village and climb the wall and leave the Last Forests. Head straight to the Dead city and find Kenya corps." Madame Oakeress handed Rain a Key card. "This will get you into every room in Kenya corps. When I left Kenya corps, I took it from a security guard because I knew either me or someone else would have to kill the Junaks. Take some friends with you. You don't want get caught by a Junak alone, their bright blue eyes can hypnotize you as they feed on your flesh." Madame Oakeress held Rain's hand "One more thing. Rain, reincarnation. The soul only goes as far as to the superior minds in the animal kingdom each lifetime. Humans are the brightest of the stars, so just be careful of your friends, you don't know who Kenya may have become. Rain you must go now, this all has to end tonight, for the Junaks are getting closer to finding us." Madame Oakeress hugged Rain. "Be careful." Madame Oakeress said. Rain dried her eyes and put the key card in her bag. "I will do my best." Rain said as she left. she knew the one person that would be willing to go with her on this journey was, Jillian.

Rain walked back through the trail, thinking about everything Madame Oakeress told her. Rain was filled with anxiety and fear, for she knew that she may die on this journey. When she got back to the festival, she quickly searched for Jillian. "Hey, Rain how did everything go?" Jillian asked as she ran up to Rain. "Let's go somewhere Quiet." Rain replied.

They walked to the very back of the festival, and Rain told her everything. "This is a lot to take in, are you sure what she said is true?" Jillian asked. "yes, it's true." Rain pulled out the key card and showed it to Jillian. "Wow, the world was just slammed on you like that? Over a simple symbol in the stars." Jillian said. "Jillian, will you please come with me?" Rain asked as she started to sob. Jillian looked at her and put her hand on her shoulder. "'til death." Jillian said as she hugged Rain.

They gathered things they thought they would need to take on the journey, for they did not know how long it would take to get to the Dead city. While gathering weapons, they came across Shelly and Olive. "Look Rain I know we haven't been the best of friends." shelly started to say but was quickly interrupted by Rain. "Shelly, now really isn't the time, I have to leave the village tonight."

"Where you going? Are going to jump the wall?" Asked Shelly. "Is that really your business, Shelly because as far as I know, you just want to know what I'm up to, so you can put me down." Rain said frustrated. "I'm not trying to do that to you anymore I just don't have a lot of friends because of my attitude, and I want to make it up to you." Shelly replied. Rain looked at Shelly and saw the sadness in her eyes. "I'm sorry. Yes, I'm trying to get to the Dead city." Said Rain feeling like a fool. "We can get you there." Said Olive. Rain looked at them for a moment, closed her eyes and thought of all things that could go wrong. She knew that they were strong and brave, but she didn't know if she could trust them. Then again trust isn't really a strong word anymore. "How?" Rain asked "We go out there quite often just to get away for a while. We have only gone during the day because we don't know what could be out there during the night, if anything it's better to have a few friends go along with you." Olive replied. "We have to go tonight, and we really could use the help." Said Rain. "We will get our things and meet you back here." Shelly said as her and Olive left quickly. "Do you think they will come back" Asked Jillian. "Yes. I can feel it in their hearts." Rain replied.

Jillian, knew at that moment that they were all about to embark on a very dangerous journey that may cost them their lives. She felt scared and unsure of her willingness to go with Rain, but she knew she had to because her friend needed her more than she could ever need someone.

"Are you really willing to go with me?" Rain asked.

"I'm scared but I will not let you down, the world can try to bring you down, but I will be there to help you up." Jillian replied.

"That means a lot." Said Rain.

Rain, grabbed her spear and checked the arrow head to make sure it was sharp, as Jillian and she waited for Olive and Shelly. Rain, thought about what Madame Oakeress had said about reincarnation and how the soul only seeks the highest intellect. This would indicate that Kenya became human again, and that's why Madame Oakeress said for Rain to be aware of her friends Kenya could be anyone, but this leaves the question will the new Kenya have the same memories, and will she still fall in the same malicious ways? Rain didn't tell anyone this she kept it to herself in case, she had told the wrong person. Rain decided to put it in the back of her mind but to keep a sharp eye on everyone just in case one of them is Kenya.

"Rain, they're coming." Jillian said as Olive and shelly came running back to them. Rain looked and saw Olive run up to her "Hey, you girls ready." Olive asked them. Rain and Jillian both nodded their heads. "follow us." Said Olive as she smiled in excitement. They walked to the great wall about a mile away from the festival. The wall was huge and higher than any of the trees within it. Rain looked at Shelly "How do we get up there?" Rain asked. "We climb the ropes." Shelly replied as she pulled out two long ropes with deer antlers tied to them. Shelly handed one of them to Olive, they both threw them at the top of the wall and hooked them in the cracks. "Now just watch how we do it, we'll wait for you at the top, so we can all climb down safely." Shelly told Rain and Jillian. Shelly and Olive started to climb as Rain and Jillian watched them pull themselves deep into the darkness of the night sky until they could be seen no more. All was silent, until they heard a voice call out to them, with an echo following afterward. It was Olive's voice telling them to climb up. "come on girls we already made it to the top." Olive shouted. Jillian looked at Rain with an excited expression on her face. "Are you ready, Rain?" Jillian asked. Rain shook for a moment nervous and full of anxiety. She knew once she got passed that wall her whole life was about to change. Rain took a deep breath and exhaled slowly. "Let's go." Rain replied. Jillian started to climb first as Rain followed. As they climbed the wall the lights around them started to fade into darkness, and the sounds from the festival grew silent. Rain started to feel weak as she pulled herself up, her palms started to sweat, and her body started to shake, she was frightened that she might let go and plummet to the ground. "Hey, give me your hand." A voice said. Rain looked up and saw shelly reaching down to grab her hand while Olive and Jillian were getting ready to climb down the other side. Throughout all her worried thoughts, Rain had already made it to the top. Shelly pulled her up. "Don't be scared we are all hear to help each other." Shelly said as she smiled at Rain. "thank you." Rain said while breathing heavily. Jillian and Olive climbed down first, then Rain and Shelly. Once they reached the bottom, Olive pulled out four jars from her bag and handed them out to each of them. "shake them so the bugs will glow, these will light our way through the night." Said Olive. Everyone shook their jars, and they started to glow a bright green. Rain shined her light and gazed at the forest before them. This was it she thought to herself, my journey, my future, my destiny it all starts here. At this moment she knew that she may never see the village again and that everything she ever learned about the world she lived in will show its true form and reveal its hidden secrets. Rain, Exhaled and picked up her bag, she saw Olive shine her light toward the direction of the path her and shelly would always take, but before any of them started walking down the path, Rain, went in front of everybody and tried her best to explain to them about the Junaks "Okay everyone before we go any further, Madame Oakeress, told me that there are creatures out here known as the Junaks. They are very dangerous and very hard to kill so let no one separate from the group, I don't want to lose anyone tonight." Rain said. She had never been good at leadership and she felt a little embarrassed now that she spoke to them in such a manner. "we have seen them before but only from a safe distance we never actually encountered one up close before, I hope to never do so." Shelly responded. "How long 'til we reach the Dead city?" Rain asked. "Not long we will be there before the nights end. Just follow us." Shelly replied. All of them began to walk down the path with Shelly and Olive leading the way. The air started to get colder and the forest grew darker, while the noises of the forest began to come alive. Rain, noticed the trees had over time formed a tunnel like shape over the path with some living trees and some dead ones. The plants and flowers grew alongside the path almost as if this once use to be a road or garden like trail. "This path will lead us to the river and from there we will get on a raft Olive and I had made, and the river will take us to the dead city." Shelly told them. As rain, listened to Shelly, she looked at the trees and branches and started to realize that there was no markings and no ribbons on them to help find the way. Rian also realized that it was convenient that Shelly just happened to know the way without asking too much detail. Shelly has always been a bully toward Rain, All her life. What if what Madame Oakeress, had said was true? What if souls do only reincarnate into varied species 'til it reaches the highest intellect? What if Kenya is Shelly? Rain, started to feel she was reading too much into it, and decided to just keep her eyes open, and not think too much on the subject. "how well do you know your way around the dead city?" Rain asked. "Not too well, but Olive and I do know a few safe spots we can hide out at incase we do encounter anything dangerous." Shelly replied. As they walked deeper into the forest the air started to get colder, and the forest grew silent. Rain had felt this before, but she couldn't remember where? Rain listened to everyone talking, but a faint noise came in the back of everyone's voices like a quiet movement or a stepping sound. Something was walking quietly toward them, like a hunter stalking its prey. Rain, tuned everyone out and all she could hear were the steps coming closer and closer and closer. Rain fell behind everyone as she was filled with anxiety and fear her heart began to shake, and she realized the fear she was feeling was from a dream she had, a nightmare. The steps started coming faster and faster. "run!!!" Rain, shouted. Everyone turned around and saw Rain running to catch up with them while warning them of what was coming. They all soon saw a giant figure, behind Rain. Shelly lifted her light as Rain, stumbled and fell to the ground, the creature stopped before them

15

and stood on all fours. They all stared at the Beast, it was taller than all of them, it's feet were like giant claws with silver nails, it's skin was like human skin, it was bald with a big metal plate in its head, and had giant silver teeth, and big blue eyes that were glowing bright. "Don't stare into its eyes that's how it draws you in." Rain Said suddenly. None of them could move, they were all in shock. It growled loud and roared like nothing they had ever heard before. "it's a Junak." Rain whispered to herself. Jillian, lifted her spear and launched it at the Junak, it moved quickly and caused her to miss. The Junak, ran toward them, Olive climbed a tree and watched to get a clear shot at it. the Junak, stopped ready to pounce at them. Rain, jumped to the left side of the Junak, as shelly, got on the right. Jillian, stayed in the center not knowing what to do, she was shaking. "I can do this." Jillian kept telling herself while she closed her eyes. Jillian slowly pulled out her stone dagger as she opened her eyes and launched herself into the Junak. Rain and shelly, ran up to the Junak, With their spears in hand. Jillian stabbed the Junak in the chest as it swung its left claw at her face causing her fly into the forest where she hit the ground and rolled down a giant hill deep into the darkness. Rain and Shelly, kept fighting the Junak. Rain, saw the metal plate in the Junaks head, and saw Olive on the tree above the beast. "you have to hit it in the head, break the metal plate!!!" Rain, shouted. Olive saw the plate in its head and thought for a moment how she was going to do it, but she didn't have enough time to come up with a positive solution on how to break the metal plate. So, she decided to hit it in the center of the head and break its skull. Olive dived off the tree and landed on top of the Junak, she stabbed her spear in to its skull as hard as she could, but the Junak pulled her off its back, with its giant claw and ripped off her leg. Olive screamed in agony as Rain and shelly tried to fight the Junak. Rain and Shelly were both knocked aside, As Olive pulled out her stone dagger and tried her hardest to fight knowing this might be her last night alive. The Junak ripped off her arm and sliced open her stomach, feeding upon her intestines, and killing her. Rain, pulled out her stone dagger and ran toward the Junak. She slid under it before the Junak could grab her and sliced its throat, blood splattered as she moved out of the way. The Junak fell to the ground, and its eyes began to close. Rain, took a deep breath, her body was still shaking and covered in perspiration. Shelly ran toward Olives body kneeled and caressed her remains. Shelly, was sobbing as she shouted toward the night sky. "I loved her!! You took her away from me!!" Rain, walked up to Shelly and held her, Shelly lade her head on Rains side as she cried. Rain stared at olives remains and began to weep. "Where is Jillian?" Shelly asked. Rain raised her head remembered where Jillian had fallen. "I have to find her." She said in a panic. Rain ran to the area she saw her last and ran into the darkness she got to the hill where Jillian had tumbled down, and started calling out her name, but there was no answer. Rain started to cry as she kept calling. Rain didn't know what to do anymore, all she knew is that she had to keep going but her heart told her Jillian might be alive. Rain saw shelly running toward her. "Rain, we have to keep going something is happening to the blood of that creature." Shelly told her frightenedly. Rain knew what was happening, they didn't kill the Junak, and it was developing a new body. Rain lifted her spear and stabbed it into the ground on top of the hill in the hopes that if Jillian is alive she will have an idea of where to go. Rain and Shelly ran back toward the Junaks body, the new body was still in the prosses of development. Shelly quickly untied a ribbon from Olives neck and took it with her as she guided Rain through the rest of the path. They both ran as fast as they could, and the forest got darker and the air got colder. "How long 'til we get to the raft?" Rain asked. "Not long, we are getting closer." Shelly replied. Rain followed Shelly through the darkness of the forest neither one of the them were warriors, Rain knew this by heart, but at this moment when all unsuspecting situations come about, when all other options are closed, and a blind eye opens to a dark reality and the only option you have is to give your best shot at bringing in the light only then will you be a true warrior. Rain thought of this and kept these words close to her heart, knowing she is vulnerable to this world her and her friends are now in. Rain could hear something not too far from them it was like a whooshing sound, it got louder as they drew closer to it, water. It was water, Rains eyes grew big they made it to the river. Shelly stopped running once they made it to the edge of the river, they both looked for the raft shelly and olive had built. The raft was tied to an old branch that was stuck in the mud just a few feet from where they had arrived. Shelly untied the raft and stopped for a second and looked at Rain. "What if we don't make it back?" she asked. Rain took a moment to answer, still breathing heavily from running, a tear dripping from her eye, right now all she could feel was emotional pain. "Shelly just know that you were at one point my enemy but right now you are my friend. I will be by your side, live or die you are my friend." Shelly raised her head up as she finished untying the raft. "I'm glad you are." She said. Rain was about to get on the raft with shelly, when she stopped and reached into the pocket of her bag and pulled out the flower Jillian had given to her before the festival, the flower was a little torn but still presentable, she tied a ribbon around it and hung it from a tree as she whispered softly to herself. "I know you are alive, I can feel your pain, this flower will help guide you, I love you my sister." Rain and shelly got on the raft and sailed in to the night.

Deep in the darkness of the forest where fear and death go without mercy, where Junaks roam free to feed on its prey. Jillian's body rests at the bottom of a steep hill, with her clothes tattered and torn, and her body covered in lesions while bleeding profusely. Jillian awoke, the ground was damp the air was cold, and Jillian's body wet and soaked with what she realized was her own blood. She kept her eyes closed because she was scared to find out what happened to her. all she knew was that she was in so much pain, she tried to move her left arm and excruciating pain came soaring threw her body as she screamed loud in agony. Jillian wished she didn't have to look at herself while she still had her eyes closed she felt her left arm creeping her hand gently down she felt the bone sticking out of her forearm, Jillian gasped in pain and fright, she opened her eyes only to discover she is now blind. She felt her face it was coved in blood with three giant scratches that stretched across her face, the scratches started from her left temple and left cheek bone across her eyes to her right cheek. Jillian started to cry for she now knew what it was like to be a step away from death. She thought to herself what might have happened to the others, did the same get bestowed upon them as well or did they suffer a much worse fate, no, She, did not want to think that, Rain was smarter than this, Rain would have found a way out, somehow someway they are all okay. Jillian always felt she wasn't perfect that no matter how hard she tried she would always fail, her anxieties always got the best of her it was just a part of who she is, and now she lays wounded crippled by her own courage, punished for her own actions, she feels like a failure at everything she is in life, and longs for death. She stops and cleanses her anger and sadness and she understands that she is more than that, there is still time she can find her friends, she can make it through this tough road she now travels, and she can prove to herself that her life is worth saving even if she is so close to death, at her weakest point she will be the strongest. Jillian lifted herself up from the ground, the pain kept coming in waves, but she felt strong enough to stand and she could not see but she could hear, and she could feel that was all she needed. Jillian took one step and she stumbled but kept her stance, she began to walk and each step she took didn't go without staggering. Jillian raised her head to the sky, she never believed in God she wasn't even sure if reincarnation was real, all she knew was that at this moment she needed a little bit of hope. She spoke in a whispered prayer "To whomever it may concern, me and my friends, lives are at stake. Our, journey has only just begun, and we are disbanded, I do not know where they are now. But I feel they are still alive. I am weak, wounded, and blind please if anyone is out there if anyone cares to listen help me find my friends." Jillian began to cry as she thought of Rains beautiful smile and all the memories they shared together. As Jillian carefully dried her eyes she felt a hand rest upon her right shoulder and a man's voice spoke. "I am zero, I will be your eyes."

Rain, stared into the river while she Compton plated all that has happened, she had a million questions and no one to answer them. She was searching her whole life for what she was meant to be, but this is not what she ever thought she would be, a possible hero or failure. Rain feared the future, and what it might hold, but as a human she was always curious. Her future is here and now, and she must figure out how to go through it or at least build the confidence to do her best. Shelly used a long tree branch to row the boat down the river, the current was calm and quiet as Shelly gazed into the starlit night with eyes watery and a heart filled with pain. "I can't do this!" Shelly shouted. Rain turned and looked at Shelly. "I know it's hard, I understand what you are going through." Rain replied. "No, you don't!" Shelly shouted again. At that moment she knew what shelly meant, it wasn't about embarking on this journey Shelly has more courage than Rain could ever have, Shelly was in mourning. "Rain. Oh god, I loved her. She was everything to me, my best friend the light of my life. We were going to have a home together I promised her that…. I promised Olive a lot of things that will never happen now." Rain walked up to shelly and put her arm around her. "Rain, Olive used to tell me that she would always be my light in the dark, that no matter how hard things got, she would be there. She would also say that no matter what problems came are way we're going to make it…. Olive, we're going to make it." Shelly laid her head on Rains shoulder as she continued to sob. "Olive, loved you, we all knew that. She will always be a part of you cherish her memory. she was a warrior." Rain said caringly. "Rain, I know Jillian is alive I feel it in my heart." Shelly said. "I feel it too." Rain replied. Shelly and Rain both gazed into the stars, the moon was full, and the stars were bright. Rain let go of shelly and walked to the other side of the raft. "What's wrong?" Shelly asked. "We have to find a way to kill the Junaks." Rain Replied. "We will, there has to be something we can do." Shelly said. "That's the whole point. That is why We are out here, to kill them, Kenya corps holds the answer to killing them that's my destiny, I was sent out to kill them and free everyone from this world we now live in. there was no nuclear explosion, we were taught to believe that, so we wouldn't leave the village. If we did, we would become victim to the Junaks. Madame Oakeress told me that I was the one to rise and save the world. Why me? Who am I to be the one to do this? I'm just a simple girl living a basic life in the village, and now at random I'm destined to save the world I couldn't even save my friends. Look we can't kill the Junaks they will always multiply they create a new body each time you kill one of them. That is why this world is almost extinct. We can slow the Junaks down, but we can't kill them, only a single button in Kenya corps can do it and I don't even know where it's at or let alone what to do once we get there, all I know is that I am Scared." Rain lowered her head. "Don't be scared I'm with you, we can do this." Shelly Said. Rain smiled, she knew that shelly meant well but at this point they both felt hopeless. There was no one that could help them, all they had was each other and they weren't sure that would be enough. "When Jillian and I were little we became blood sisters, because we knew we would be friends the rest of our lives." Rain said in a soft voice, as she pulled out her stone dagger and ran it through the water. Rain walked up to Shelly. "If we die, we die sisters in honor and friendship." Rain said as she sliced her right hand. Shelly felt honored and stuck out her left hand. "Until I die you are my sister." Shelly said as Rain sliced her hand. They both pressed their wounded hands together binding their blood. They both stared into each other's eyes and knew what it truly meant to feel honor in the eyes of a warrior. The current started to pick again shelly and Rain watched as they passed the end of the forest and saw a land of dirt and mountains. The mountains stood tall and was covered in grass, small trees and plant life and the highest peak graced the sky. Rain had never seen such a beautiful site in her life. She wondered what life must have been like before the Junaks came around, before Kenya ruled the world. Kenya such an evil person, Rain thought to herself. How could someone destroy something so beautiful, what was Kenya thinking? what would come to please her intentions? Why? Rain knew somehow, she would figure this all out. If Kenya did reincarnate into another human being, Rain just hoped that they don't fall into the same malicious ways of Kenya. Rain, stared into the mountains and imagined people and all kinds of animals walking through them, just to see it alive, to see love in it. The world can be so beautiful if we just gave it a chance. why does it have to die? The earth graced us with the gift of life and opportunity, and Kenya wanted to conquer and destroy it, to take a beautiful flower and close it in the palm of her hand until it suffocates and dies. "We're here." Shelly said as they saw the mountains end and saw empty space, but out in the distance they saw the remains of a dead city. Rain was speechless she had never seen a city before she had seen pictures Madame Oakeress kept in her hut, but this is the first time she ever seen one in real life. Shelly and Rain drew closer and Rain could vaguely see the details of the buildings. The buildings were dark from the night sky, they looked old and as if life hadn't been there for years. As the raft drew closer and closer Rain could see the buildings had shattered windows, broken sections and black marks and plant life all over them. Rain realized she was seeing a life extinct. Shelly rowed the raft to a nearby dock. "Welcome to the dead city." Shelly said as she hooked a rope to a post and tied it to the raft. "It's so hollow, and lifeless." Rain responded. "I never said it would be pretty, I just said I would get you here." Shelly replied. Rain grabbed her bag, and looked at Shelly, Rain knew in her heart that she could trust her with her life and now regrets the doubt she had felt once before. Madame Oakeress taught all the girls in the village how to trust their instincts, to believe in the warm feeling in their hearts because it always gives your conscience the right answer. Shelly and rain climbed the ladder and stood on the dock as they gazed into the darkness of the dead city, Silent was the night and neither one them knew what terror will be beheld in the rest of their journey. "Stay beside me and do not let yourself get distracted by anything until we have reached a safe spot." Shelly told Rain. "I promise Shelly." Rain said. They both grabbed their things and walked into the darkness of the dead city.

Jillian still at the bottom of the hill scared and concerned. "Your name is Zero? Why do you want to help me?" She asked. "Because you need it. Yes, that is my name. I saw your friends and how they fought the Junak." He responded. "Did they live? Are they okay?" She asked anxiously. "Yes except for one, she had black hair and she was on a tree." He replied. "Olive!!! What happened to her?" Jillian asked in fright. "She passed away. I'm sorry." He said. Jillian cried, trying to stay strong, but to mourn a death is so hard. "What happened to the Junak?" She asked. "They slowed it down, but it developed a new body and wandered into woods. Look I can help you find your friends, do you know where they were headed?" Zero asked. "The dead city." Jillian said. Zero paused and thought about it. "To find Kenya Corps?" Zero asked. "yes." Jillian said as she started to stumble. Zero caught her fall. "You have lost a lot of blood." He said. Jillian felt very hazy and weak. "What do you look like?" she asked to distract herself from the damaged state she was in. "I am a cyborg, Half man half robotic organism." Zero responded. "I don't understand." Jillian said. Zero put one of his hands in Jillian's right hand "Do you feel it?" He asked as Jillian felt his hand it felt metallic and she felt his other hand and it felt human but wounded almost like the skin started decay. She felt the rest of his body and some parts were metal while others were flesh, cold dead flesh. She felt his face his forehead had metal, but his nose, and cheeks were skinless. She stopped in fright "What happened to you?" She asked. "I am a failed test of Kenya Corps. Kenya tested many different projects and one of them was if she could prolong life although she was raised to believe in reincarnation just like I was, she was frightened of death. Kenya wanted some way to survive, so she and her scientists started to develop ways to create cyborg bodies and see if they would out live human existents, so she could become one in later years, but she needed a Gennie pig, I was the lucky one. I denied her request and She grew with such anger as I turned away from her, the last thing I remember was feeling a gunshot to my back as I passed out, and three months later I awoke as a cyborg. She was right... a cyborg can out live human existents, even its own human body, only the robotic part of me is alive." Zero stopped. "How could she do this to you?"

Jillian asked. "Kenya asked me because I'm the one person who can't deny her request." Zero responded. "What do you mean?" Jillian asked. "Kenya was my mother. I can't remember her face, and I can't remember her ever being kind all I know is that she is responsible for all that has happened to the world, and I sadly was her son and one of her soldiers before the Junaks took over." Zero said as he exhaled. Jillian stood in awe, her heart was racing, but she knew throughout all that has happened this person or cyborg is her only means of salvation. Will she ever find her friends? Will she get to help them on the rest their quest? Jillian has no answers, but she knows that Zero is here for her and he may be able to give her the answers through the journey. "I'm so sorry for what has happened to you. It seems as though we have both met a fate worse than death." Jillian said. "Death is beautiful, peaceful, I long for it. Death is a chance to escape the pain and burden that life brings, but we wait for our time of dying. The best thing to do is to live your life to the fullest you'll have your time of enjoyment and your time of suffering just remember to be who you are and do what makes you happy, so death is welcoming for it has no predictions." Zero replied. "Please help me find my friends, Zero. I need to help them." Jillian said as she started to weep. "I will get you to them, with all my power, but we have to go now." Zero told her. Jillian put out her hand out and Zero held it as he guided her slowly to the top of the hill Jillian struggled to walk and she found it incredibly difficult to not physically see what she was doing, each step was like walking on the edge of a cliff with loose, dirt at any moment she could lose her balance. Jillian was scared more scared than she had ever been, but she fought hard not to let it get in the way of her confidence, her courage. Jillian still felt blood dripping down her forearm. "stop." She said. Zero watched as Jillian painfully struggled to rip a piece of cloth from her skirt. "Here... ah... my... arm wrap it for me" she said as she started breathing heavily and nervously, she handed the cloth to Zero. Her heart raced while she awaited intense agony. Zero carefully pushed her bone back into her flesh and wrapped her arm tightly to keep pressure on it. Jillian gasped and screamed, and she couldn't help groaning and grinding her teeth from the heavy pain soaring through her body. Tears dripping heavily from her eyes as she took a deep breath and exhaled. Her heart calmed, and she started feel the pain come to a warm pause, where it still hurt but she can manage. "this won't help you much, but it will do for now, I'm very concerned about your loss of blood, you may need serious medical attention, or in terms of your culture, you may need a healer." Zero said as he stared at her wounded arm. "I don't care about my condition right now I, I, I just want to find my friends, even if it kills me. I need to know that they are okay." Jillian said. "don't worry we will find them." Zero replied as he took Jillian s hand and walked with her to the top of the hill. Zero saw something at the very top, his robotic eye examined the object as his analysis read it was a weapon, used to impale or puncture victims, and preys. A spear. "Jillian, there is a spear in the ground it may belong to one of your friends." Zero said. "Zero please bring it to me." She replied. Zero grabbed the spear and put it in Jillian's hand. Jillian dropped it on the ground and fell on her knees, while keeping her broken arm curled in a ball she used her right hand to feel everywhere she could until she touched the spear, she moved her hand up and down the spear and felt something at the end of it, it was a ribbon. She held the loose ends of the ribbon tightly. Jillian felt her eyes water up again and she smiled, a light smile but it was something she had not felt in a long time. "Rain, you're alive. You're alive. I promise I'll find you." Jillian said softly as she lifted the spear and held it against her chest. "Zero, Rain left this here to guide me to her. This hill leads us to the path that will take us to the river." Jillian told him. Zero helped her up. "Then we must go to the river. If we encounter a Junak, I do not want you to try and fight while in such a vulnerable state I will protect you." Zero told her. Jillian knew he was right but if the situation comes about she may have to take a chance, but for now it is best to stay safe. "I understand, thank you, Zero." Jillian replied. They walked through the brush and the trees and found their way to the path. Zero discovered the remains of the Junak and Olives body. Zero informed Jillian about Olives remains "Take me to her body, Zero, Please?" Jillian said softly. Zero walked her to Olives body, and Jillian got down on her knees and felt Olives face Jillian whispered a soft song from the village. "In our dreams we can stand by the ocean, in the sand. Sleep in the stars to forget all the scars, when we awake we will remember what was, ours. Rest well my sister I'll see you again." Jillian kissed her index and middle finger and placed them on Olives forehead, then closed Olives eyes. Zero helped Jillian up. "what were those words you were whispering to her." Zero asked. "Those are the words of my village, we say them to the sisters that pass away. In my village love is a powerful word it's more than getting together with someone or caring for your family It's friendship it's helping the people around you. like them or hate them you will know this person the rest of your life and to know someone is not to judge someone it's to understand them and the journey they share with you." Jillian took a breath. "Your very strong in your beliefs, I wish I could feel the same, but darkness takes over me just a little too much, if only I could wash it all away, leave this forsaken life. I'm really a mess, I am nothing, just a failed project and I'm alone. I want to leave this behind and find my peace, to rest, I have gone on for too long now, I just want my peace." Zero looked at Jillian and took her hand, they walked down the path and the forest was silent. Jillian thought about what Zero said and just understood him like second nature, Zero, was like her in the ways of suffering and in the ways of emotional, and physical stress, that they are both victims of an unfortunate fate and now they must live out their lives behind the scars. Jillian held on to Zero's hand as tight as she could so maybe that will give him a feeling that she cares about him. Zero stopped walking he listened carefully. "What's wrong?" Jillian asked. "Just be very quiet." Zero replied. He lifted the spear, all was dark, all was silent. A scratching sound came in faint waves as if an animal was about to pounce on its prey. Jillian was shaking, she didn't know what to do if a Junak should come about. "Here." Zero said as he put the spear in Jillian's hand. "what about you?" Jillian asked. "Don't worry I've never needed it before. It will protect you if I should die." Zero replied. The scratching turned into an animal running at high speed the animal roared loud and another roar followed behind it and at that moment Jillian knew the Junaks were coming. Jillian held out her spear not sure what direction to be in and Zero stood in front of her. One Junak leaped out of the trees as Zero jumped in the air bent his robotic wrist down and a metal spike came out of his arm as he jammed it in the side of the Junaks throat as they both fell to the ground. The second Junak leaped out of the trees, landing in front of Jillian, while Zero and the other Junak were still fighting. The Junak got close enough to Jillian it could smell the perspiration and fear off her. Jillian was beyond scared she was blind and death was staring her in the face. The Junak shined its bright blue eyes to hypnotize her. Jillian was wondering what it was going to do to her, how it was going to kill her, how much it was going to hurt, and why was it taking so long for the Junak to do something, but then the thought hit her. Rain said the Junak will try to hypnotize its prey before The Junak kills it, but she is blind. The Junak can't hypnotize her because she can't see. Jillian payed attention to the Junaks breathing to get an idea of how high the Junak stood, when she figured it out she lifted her spear as fast as she could and stabbed the Junak in the eye by lucky chance. The Junak lifted its self-up with Jillian still hanging from the spear as it fell on its back to the ground Jillian got up and just kept stabbing it without pulling the spear out of its eye until she felt the spear go through the skull. The Junak stopped moving. Jillian pulled out the spear and heard Zero still fighting the other Junak. Zero was under the Junak, it was clawing at his robotic shoulder trying to keep his spike down, but Zero used all his strength and pushed it off him launching the Junak into the air, but it landed on all fours and ran back at him. "C'mon you fucking mutt, come kill me!!!" Zero shouted angrily. The Junak jumped and Zero slid under it slicing it from its chest to its groin. Zero watched as the Junak landed on all fours again, but this time it looked back at Zero, it tried to turn, but once it did, the Junaks chest and stomach split wide open and its intestines spewed out, as it fell to the ground. "Zero!! are you okay?" Jillian shouted. "Yes, but we must keep moving, the Junaks Are beginning to multiply, and we don't have much time." Zero said. "Okay, I'm just glad you are alright." Jillian said as Zero took her spear and her hand and they both ran toward the river.

The Junaks blood oozed out of the Body as it started to thicken and take form of another Junak enclosed in tissue and a skin like sack. The newly born Junak grew to its adult form as it tore through the bloody sack with its claws until it was free, and it let out it's loud roar as the second Junak tore through its sack and growled menacingly. Both newly born Junaks looked at each other walked in rotation eyeing their likeness they both let out howls to signify that they are one of the same and now join forces to create a new pack of Junaks. The Junaks, listened carefully to hear for sounds of future prey, the sounds they heard were west of them deep in the woods near the river. The Junaks roared and ran towards the river.

Zero and Jillian ran as fast they could, they could hear water running down stream. Zero knew it was just a matter of time before they reached the river. Jillian was struggling to catch her breath, her heart was racing, but she couldn't stop she couldn't let her self-quit no matter how weak she felt this is her destiny. They reached the river. Zero, searched for wood anything to build a raft but was to no avail, Jillian slowly caught her breath. "what do we do now, Zero?" She asked. "I Can't find anything to help build a raft. We may be able to cross the river and follow it down stream to the dead city, but it will slow us down." Zero replied. "If this is our only option, then it must be done." Jillian said as she took a step backward and touched a tree branch as she felt it she felt something hanging from it, she grabbed it, the object felt soft, it was a flower. Jillian, realized it was the flower she had given to Rain before the festival. Jillian held on to it for a moment, she was getting closer to finding, Rain, and Shelly. Jillian placed the flower in her pocket, and told herself that when she finds Rain, she will return it. She heard animals running, coming fast toward them. "they're coming, Zero!" Jillian shouted. Zero looked back toward the forest and saw the Junaks out in the distance. "We have to go, now!!" Zero shouted. He grabbed Jillian's hand and took her into the water. It was cold, and the force of the water flow was making it hard for them to walk. The Junaks arrived at the riverside, roaring loud with glowing eyes of blue fire. Zero turned and saw the Junaks diving into the water and swimming toward them. Zero let go of Jillian's hand. "stay back!" He said to Jillian, as he put her spear in her hand. Jillian could hear the splashing of the water as the Junaks came swimming fast. Zero bent his wrist and the spike out of his forearm, the Juanks both leaped out of the water plummeting down on Zero and Jillian. As Zero and one of the Junaks sank into the water, Zero, stabbed his spike into the bottom of the Junaks jaw forcing the spike into the Junak's inner mouth into its head as it fought hard clawing at his chest trying to force him down to the bottom of the water Zero was pulling with all his might and caused his spike to break through the Junaks face. Zero forced the Junaks body off him, and he rose from the water. "Jillian!!!" He shouted. Jillian was nowhere in sight. "Jillian!!!" He shouted again. He looked around and saw water splashing not too far from where he was. Zero swam as fast as he could to save Jillian. Jillian was deep in the water as the Junak stood on top of her with its claws forcing her down. Jillian was stabbing at its legs although she could not see she gave her best efforts. Jillian's spear broke in the Junak's leg. Jillian let go of the broken piece of the spear and felt for anything that could be used as a weapon. Jillian felt something that felt like a rope made of rubber, she pulled it but part of it was stuck in the ground. The Junak lowered its head and bit into her stomach. Jillian screamed in agony losing her breath and she used the end of the rope she had found and wrapped it around the Junaks neck the best she could, not knowing what she had done, the Junak let her go and tried to free its self but drowned in the process. Jillian was floating deep in the water bleeding rapidly from her stomach. Zero reached her and pulled her head out of the water so she could breathe. "Jillian! Oh god. Jillian you're going to be okay." He said to her as he swam with her in his arm to shore. When Zero got to shore he laid Jillian on the ground, she was unconscious. Zero preformed C.P.R on her and Jillian started to cough up water and blood. Zero exhaled. "I thought I lost you." He said calming down from fright. "I… am… hurt really bad." Jillian said in a troubled voice. Zero examined her body and saw her stomach with a large chunk of flesh torn from it, and it was bleeding severely. "Jillian, you have lost too much blood. Your wound is too deep. I… I can't save you." Zero said as he started to sob. "don't worry just try to get me to Rain." Jillian said as she placed her hand on her stomach. "I have to find something for you to cover the wound." Zero said as he ran into the forest to find anything he could, he knew he didn't have much time. He looked high and low to find a cloth or tattered rag, just something to help slow the bleeding. He came across old remains of animals and humans, but the clothes on the humans were long since deteriorated from time. He ran a little further and came across a giant object in the darkness its shape was in the form of a fighter jet. He examined it with his cybernetic eye, and to his surprise it was still intact and fully operational although the windshield was smashed. Zero ran up to the fighter jet and opened the hatch, a dead corps sat in the jet with its skull crushed in. Zero looked at the dead soldier's dog tag. "Well, officer Derek Murkem, I'm going to have commandeer your shuttle craft. You fought well soldier rest in peace." Zero said as he lifted the soldiers body out of the jet and laid him on the ground. Zero got in the jet and looked at the controls, and turned it on, he lifted the jet into the air and flew it to the river where Jillian lays dying. Zero arrived at the river and saw several Junaks heading toward Jillian's body. He figured out how to fire the weapons and shot every Junak insight. Zero landed the jet as gently as he could without letting down the wheels, so they would be able to climb in without a ladder. Once he landed he jumped out of the jet and ran to Jillian. "Jillian!" He shouted. Zero started to lightly tap her face to wake her up. "Jillian, c'mon baby girl wakeup." He continued. "Don't die on me now." Jillian moved her hand and started to murmur "I'm... uh, still here." She said in a whisper. "oh my god, thank you. Huh, I'm going to get you to them." Zero said as he sobbed. Zero lifted her up and held her as tight as he could without hurting her. He had never cared for someone before, but at this moment he felt like he was about to lose the closest friend he ever had, for Zero had lived in this dead world alone. Zero placed her in the backseat, he held her hand for a moment and then placed it over her stomach to cover her wound. Zero got in the front seat and flew the jet into the air and headed for the dead city.

Rain, and Shelly stood in the shadows of the night, hidden within the dead city. Rain and shelly stood by a broken-down building, looking at all the old cars and stores that use to service civilians. There was dead rotting carcasses of humans and animals lying everywhere they looked, discarded garbage, and fragments of what once was, the dead city lay a wasteland. Junaks walk through the roads, roaming for prey, digging through trash cans, breaking through windows of buildings to see what hides within them. Rain, and Shelly watched and waited for the Junaks to walk far enough away to give them a chance to sneak into one of the buildings to search for better means of protection. "I'll go first than I'll give the signal for you to follow, okay?" Shelly told Rain. "Okay just be careful." Rain replied. They watched as several Junaks passed by them. Rain and shelly kept their backs against the wall of the building hiding them in the darkness, as Junaks walked by observantly, looking at everything in sight. Luckily, they did not see Rain and shelly. Once they passed by, Shelly peaked out from there hiding place and saw that it was clear. "Alright, I'm going." She said to Rain. Shelly ran quietly to the other side of the road to the next building. When she got to the next building, she looked at the road, she saw two Junaks walking by, and signaled Rain to wait. The Junaks passed by sniffing and snarling as they roamed the streets, deep into the city. Shelly signaled Rain, and Rain looked at both sides of the road to see if it was clear, as she made her way across, with her dagger in hand. When Rain got there shelly put her finger to her mouth. "be very quiet, we have to sneak into the building and see if we can find weapons."

Shelly whispered. "what if the door is locked?" Rain asked. "I can open it, but we have to be very quiet and discrete, Okay?" Shelly replied. They looked toward the road and saw it was clear, and they made their way to the door of the building. The doors were made of glass with metal frames around them, the sign on the door read Pawn shop. "Keep an eye out Okay? I'm going to do this as quickly and quietly as possible." Shelly said "Okay." Said Rain. Shelly lifted her leg and kicked the doors wide open shattering the glass and making a loud crashing sound. "Okay, let's go." Shelly said as she walked in. "Very subtle, Shelly." Rain said sarcastically. The inside of the building was dark, there were objects all over the walls and rows of things surrounding the area. "What is all this stuff?" Shelly asked. "I'm not sure." Rain replied. They walked all round looking for weapons, they came across all sorts of power tools, jewelry, leather bags, cameras, guitars, and movies. Rain and Shelly had no idea what any of these things were the only things they were looking for were weapons, spears, or daggers something that would help them on their journey. Rain walked toward a wall, where there hung a giant sword, with a long silver blade, with intertwining tribal markings engraved in it. the handle was gold and was covered in amber and sapphire diamond studs. The sign near the sword read that it was an authentic model sword of the ancient warriors. Rain carefully lifted the sword off the stand, and held it with both hands, amazed by the beauty of it. The ancient warriors must have been powerful, to be graced with such a beautiful weapon, Rain thought to herself. "Shelly, did you find a weapon?" Rain asked. Shelly walked up to her holding a Katana sword. "Yes." Shelly replied. A sound came from outside the building, both Shelly and Rain raised their swords and stared at the window as three Junaks came crashing in and ran toward them. Rain and Shelly lifted their swords and ran toward the Junaks yelling as they dived into battle with the great beasts. The Junaks were roaring and slashing their claws at the two women. Rain Slashed at one of the Junaks, the Junak pounced at her as she moved to the side and sliced its front leg. The Junak roared loud in pain as another Junak came up from behind Rain and slashed her back. Rain screamed in pain and she spun around in a sudden race of panic slashing the first Junaks throat and cutting the other Junaks head off. She ran toward Shelly to help her fight off the other Juank. Shelly kept her sword up as the Junak approached her, The Junak jumped into the air, as Shelly stuck out her sword and the Junak landed on top of it impaling itself on the blade, while Shelly and the Junak both fell to the ground. Rain pushed the Junak off Shelly and helped her up. "Shelly, are you alright." Rain asked. "yeah, I'm okay. Rain, your back?" Shelly said. "yeah, I know, I'll be fine." Said Rain. They were both breathing heavily. "We have to keep moving. Shelly, do you know where Kenya corps could be?" Rain asked. "No, but I know where we can look at a map." Shelly responded. "Where?" Rain asked. "Not far, follow me." Shelly said. They both ran to the door and looked outside, the road was clear. They ran down the road as quick as they could, eyes wide open, hearts racing if a Junak should be waiting they will be prepared. Rain followed Shelly as they ran, passing by old grocery stores, clothing stores, barbershops, and giant office buildings, with a few restaurants here in between. They stopped at a bus stop with a bench and a billboard behind it. "Here, this is it." Shelly said. Rain looked at the billboard, it was a map of the whole city. Rain had no idea how to read a map, she was never given the opportunity. Rain looked at it and tried to figure it out, but she turned away feeling like she didn't understand, and saw the stop sign on the corner. The sign read that they are by Cortez St. and markets St. She looked at the map and saw the same names on there. She began to trace the line with her finger, the line led through the first half of the city to the countryside, and to the other half of the city and there they saw an outline of a building that had the name Kenya corps on it. "How far is that?" Rain asked. "I'm not sure maybe about ten miles." Shelly said. "Okay, this will be the best way to get there." Rain told her. They ran down Cortez St. and passed several vehicles, knocked over trash cans, and mail boxes, but Shelly kept looking at the vehicles and started to realize that humans used them as a means of transportation. She saw a two-wheeled vehicle, big enough to hold two people on it. Shelly stopped. "Rain, do you think that still works?" She asked. "I don't know. what is it?" Rain asked. They both walked and read the name on the side of it. It was a Bakerson motorcycle and the keys were still in the ignition. Shelly lifted the bike off its side. "Do you know how to work one of those" Rain asked. "No but I know if it works it will get us there faster." Shelly said as she started to smile. Rain was feeling nervous, she looked around and saw the skeletal remains of a person with a helmet and jacket on and holding an Ak-47 assault rifle. Rain walked to the body and took the gun out of its hand and removed its jacket, the sleeves were torn on it, so Rain ripped them off and put the jacket on to cover the wounds on her back. She tore the strap off her bag and tied it on her sword, she carried the sword on her back pulled out the key card from her bag and put it in her jacket pocket. She left the bag on the ground and took the gun with her as she got on the back of the bike with Shelly. Shelly revved the bike up it started to spit and sputter and then started to run smoothly. Shelly started driving she was swerving but eventually caught her balance, she hit a switch on the bike that turned on the front light headed down the road at high speed. Rain felt the wind hitting her as her hair flew in the breeze, she had never felt anything like it, she felt like she was flying. They rode deep into the city, passing by everything at an extreme rate. Rain looked behind and saw a herd of Junaks running after them. "They're coming!!" Rain shouted. Shelly started ridding faster as Rain pulled out her gun and fired at the Junaks. Rain had no idea how to use a gun properly, she just did her best to shoot at the Junaks. Shelly and Rain soon made it out of city limits and made it into the country side. The Junaks started gaining on them and Rain kept firing hitting several of them at a time and missing several them at a time. Rains gun soon ran out of ammo and she threw the gun at the Junaks. Shelly and Rain rode on to a bridge that was built over a giant lake. As they rode Rain pulled out her sword. "Try to keep steady!!!" She shouted to Shelly. The Junaks were only a few feet away from them, Rain could tell that there was at least twenty of them coming after her and Shelly. Rain carefully tried to stand on the bike, she finally balanced on the seat of the bike, lifted her sword and she jumped off leaping into the air high above the Junaks as she came crashing down on top of them, slashing at everything in sight. Shelly Turned the bike around and rode toward the Junaks. Shelly saw One of the Junaks staring at her she avoided its eyes as she threw herself off the bike and let it crash into the Junak. Shelly landed on the road, she got up and pulled out her sword and started fighting. Rain was slashing at all the junaks around her, as the Junaks were clawing and roaring at her. Shelly came running in, helping Rain fight them all off. Rain and Shelly diced as many as they could, hacking off heads and limbs, and before they knew it there was only two Junaks left. Rain and Shelly walked toward the Junaks, As the Junaks howled into the night. Rain lifted her sword and one of the

Junaks came at her, she slashed upward slicing the Junaks face, then stabbed it in the heart. Shelly and Rain both sliced up the other Junak. "We have to keep moving, Shelly. It won't be long before they start multiplying." Rain told her. Shelly nodded her head as she caught her breath. "We'll have to make it on foot, the motorcycle is gone." Shelly said. They both started running over the bridge, as the blood of the Junaks started developing new bodies. Rain and Shelly ran as fast as they could, not knowing what was awaiting them in the other half of the city, they just knew that they had to get there. They made it off the bridge and kept running straight, not looking back.

Zero, stared into the night, as he approached the dead city. Zero, listened carefully incase Jillian stopped breathing, he had no other thought in his head except to find Rain wherever she may be. Zero flew through the first half of the city, his cybernetic eye traced for human beings, but there was none to be insight. The jet started beeping notifying him that he is low on fuel. Zero, kept scanning for humans, as he made it to the countryside of the city. He picked up on a herd of Junaks heading for the other side of the city and picked up on a motorcycle wrecked on the road by a ton of Junak corpses. This is where they are. He thought to himself. Zero, drew closer to the Junaks and started firing. Several of the Junaks roared and started clawing as if to fight back, some leaped in to the air landing on the jet. Zero spun the jet around and crashed it into the bridge. The jet slid hitting and running over whatever Junaks remained on the road. The jet hit the rail of the bridge tail first, while Zero got out of his seat grabbed Jillian and leaped out of the jet. The jet broke the side of the bridge and fell with several Junaks still on it. The jet hit a pile of giant sharp boulders sticking out of the lake causing the jet to explode.

Rain and Shelly heard a loud explosion behind them as they turned suddenly and saw the wreckage in the distance. "what was that?" Shelly asked frightened by the sound. Rain felt fear in her heart, she couldn't bear the thought, she knew what it was, the heart never lies. "Jillian." She said. Shelly looked at her then looked back at the wreckage. They both ran back, out of breath and filled with anxiety. They saw a shadow of a figure walking toward them, the figure was at the end of the bridge. when Rain and Shelly got there, they saw a man half metal and half rotting corpse holding in his arms a weak wounded dying young woman. "Jillian!!!" Rain screamed with tears in her eyes. Rain ran up to Zero and took Jillian out of his hands. "you're going to be okay. You're going to be okay. I promise, I promise, you'll be okay." Rain, sniffled and breathed heavily with tears pouring out of her eyes and dripping onto Jillian's wounded body. Rain laid her on the ground and tore a piece of her skirt. "Shelly, wet this in the lake and bring it back to me." Rain said. Shelly took it and ran as fast as she could. Rain looked at Jillian's battered body and took off her jacket and put it over Jillian covering her wounded stomach it was bleeding every light breath Jillian took. Shelly came running back, she handed the rag to her. Rain Wiped all the blood off Jillian's face revealing her damaged eyes. "How could this happen to you? I shouldn't have ever brought you. you mean too much to me!! You couldn't even see. Please, don't die!!" Rain lifted Jillian's head and held her close. Jillian murmured and managed to pull out the flower from her pocket, and Rain took it from her hand. Jillian murmured again, Rain lowered her head to hear Jillian's voice. Jillian touched Rain's face lightly petting her cheek. "It's okay, I found you." Jillian whispered as her arm fell to the ground and her last breath exhaled as she passed away. "No!!!!" Rain screamed as loud as she could, her heart was pounding like it never had before, her face was red and covered in tears. Rain lost her best friend, her sister, the one person she spent her whole life knowing, Jillian, was gone. Shelly held Rain as she grieved, Shelly's eyes watering, the loss of hope setting in as the darkness covered their very souls. Zero walked up to them. "I am Zero, Jillian was my friend." He said. "I can help you too as I helped her." He continued. "Help me get her to the lake. please?" Rain said sniffling. Zero, Rain, and shelly lifted Jillian's body and took her to the lake. Rain placed her sword on Jillian's body and put her hands over it. "you were a strong warrior my sister, you died with honor, and great courage. The stars will watch over you. I love you." Rain Kissed her fingers and placed them on Jillian's forehead like all sisters of the village and let her body rest beneath water of the lake. "Thank you for bringing her to me." Rain said as she watched Jillian's body sink into the water. "I made her a promise." Zero said. Shelly placed her hand on Rain's shoulder. "Be strong my sister, I'm here for you." Rain raised her head and placed her hand over Shelly's. "I know." She said as she gave a little smile of gratitude with tears still in her eyes. "I'll get you to Kenya corps, but we have to leave now." Zero said. Cold was the night and the souls of the warriors withered in sadness. Rain stood up and dried her eyes, she looked at Zero, all she could feel was the numbness which pain brings to the heart. "I don't know you, I don't know what happened to you, or how you found Jillian, the only thing I do know is that you did what no one could have done. I trust you." Rain said. Zero never heard such words be put upon him, kindness is not what he is familiar with, for he spent years alone suffering with the thought of how unfair life had treated him, but with this kindness, to hear it, is to feel it. "You have the words that shed a joyful tear, but I am burdened with the death of my human side. The world can look at me however it wants and tell my story with whatever point of view it chooses, but the only person that will truly no me is myself. Jillian was my friend and the only one that understood what It means to suffer with a damaged soul, but I look not with pitied eyes but with caring eyes for she was all that I had to give me purpose, and I hope to give that same purpose to you." Zero put out his hand, Rain shook his hand and stared into his eyes and felt all the power that trust can bring. "Thank you, my friend." Rain said softly. "Follow me." Zero said as they all ran to the other half of the dead city. Rain and shelly followed Zero all through the countryside, passing trees, rotted out homes, old barbed wire fences, and rusty old vehicles. Not long after they saw the city. Zero stopped at the first building putting his back against the wall, Rain and shelly stopped, breathing heavily, not knowing what to do next. "The beasts are always watching; Kenya Corps was their home and they guard it at any cost." Zero whispered. "How far are we from Kenya Corps?" Rain asked. "About a mile." Zero replied. Shelly found a piece of rebar with a sharp end on it and handed it to Rain. "it's not much but it will help." Shelly said. Rain took it and looked at the road she could make out silhouettes of the Junaks passing by, her heart no longer beat in a race of panic, her rage and courage came in like thunder in the night. She was ready for the ultimate battle, do or die she was ready. Zero walked to the end of the building wall and peaked out to the road, then looked at Rain and Shelly. "Okay, we move quietly to the next building one at a time." Zero told them. Rain and Shelly stayed by the wall as Zero went first, Rain took a deep breath and went next, Zero, grabbed her hand when she got to the building and pulled her into the alley as Junaks came walking by. Shelly went after it was clear with her sword pulled out. They all waited

35

in the alley, in silence, then Zero finally spoke in a whisper. "Okay, when we get to Kenya Corps, you will see two big trucks, those trucks contain nothing but ammunition for guns, explosives, and fuel. I know this because I set them up carefully over the years trying not to get caught until I had enough explosives to blow this place to kingdom come. Now it feels like the time to set them off, it won't kill the Junaks but it will give you the time to get into Kenya Corps and set off all there microchips to destroy them once and for all." Zero told them. Rian lifted her weapon ready for their next move. "Let's do this." She said. Zero bent his wrist and his spike came out. "Just follow my lead." Zero looked down the road and saw it was clear but it wouldn't be for long. "Let's go" They all ran quickly down the road hiding wherever they could to keep out of the Junaks sight. They stopped by a building with a broken window, it was an old supply store. "wait here I'll be back." Zero said. Zero snuck in through the window as Rain and Shelly waited backs against the wall. "Rain, I'm worried, what if this plan doesn't work?" Shelly asked. "We keep fighting." Rain replied. Shelly kept her chin up despite her anxieties, she did her best to stay brave. Zero came back holding an orange gun. "This is a flare gun, it will fire off one shot, when I finish dumping some of the fuel make sure it hits the inside one of the trucks, okay, it will light up the night." Zero said. "what if you don't make it out?" Rain asked. "Don't worry about me." Zero replied as he handed her the gun. Zero, Rain, and Shelly started running and they saw a giant building in the distance, they had no questions, that is their destiny end Kenya Corps stood tall, and was the only building with light, and Junaks were surrounding the entire area. Rain felt hatred and rage fill her gut as they made their way to Kenya Corps. They halted by a big truck parked on the side of the road just two blocks away from Kenya Corps. Junaks started walking from all directions and pacing all around Kenya Corps "The Junaks are everywhere, no matter what we do next we are going to get caught. Are only choice being, fight 'til we reach the trucks." Zero said quietly. Shelly looked and saw several Junaks coming from behind them. "Run!!" She shouted as they all got up and ran for the trucks in front of Kenya Corps. The Junaks came running in all directions as Zero, Rain, and Shelly reached the trucks. The Junaks surrounded them as the battle began. Rain was hitting them with all her power, but a Junak snatched the rebar out of her hand and slashed her in the chest. Shelly fought and sliced as many as she could, but when she saw Rain fall to the ground she ran and decapitated the beast that attacked Rain and helped her up as Shelly continued to fight them off. Zero managed to open one of the doors to the truck closest by, got in, and started the truck to draw the Junaks attention away from Rain and Shelly. The Junaks started attacking the truck, as Rain and Shelly saw what was going on. Zero snuck through the back window of the truck to where he kept all ammunition, explosives, and fuel, he then dumped out most fuel all over floor and over the explosives. Rain and Shelly ran to the entrance of Kenya Corps, Rain looked back and saw that Zero kicked open the back doors of the truck. "Fire the gun!!!" he shouted as Junaks started jumping into the truck. Rain pointed the gun and aimed at the inside of the truck, Tears in her eyes knowing she was about to take someone's life. "Fire!!!" Zero shouted again as he fought the Junaks in the truck. Rain fired the gun and the flare shot straight into the truck lighting the fuel on fire. Rain pulled out her key card and slid it through the lock and the doors to the entrance to Kenya Corps slid open. Rain looked back and saw that Zero was still fighting the Junaks in the fire. Zero stabbed a Junak in the head and stared at its eyes "I finally have my peace." The rest of the fuel cans and explosives blew up, soon the entire truck to exploded causing the second truck to explode in complete massive destruction, with all the Junaks being blasted to bits. Rain and Shelly were blown inside Kenya Corps from the massive force of the explosion. Rain picked herself up and saw the doors of Kenya Corps close and lights came on, the whole room was white and filled with knocked over chairs, office desks, and skeletal remains. Rain turned around and she saw Shelly gasping for air and bleeding profusely. Rain ran to Shelly, falling on her knees and crying. "no, no, no, this can't happen. This can't happen. Somebody please!!! Help me!!!" Rain shouted as loud as she could but realized that there would be no answer to her cries. Shelly had a metal rod that stabbed in her horizontally entering below her ribcage and exiting through the side of her neck. Shelly's mouth was wide open as she looked at Rain and grabbed her hand, Shelly's whole body was shaking, and the floor was covered in a pool of her blood. "I'm so sorry, Shelly. I'm so Sorry." Rain said sniffling and breathing heavily. Shelly stopped gasping and her eyes and mouth closed. Rain laid beside Shelly, crying, her head pressed up against Shelly's, and still holding Shelly's hand. Rain grew dizzy as if the whole room was rotating around her and Shelly. She didn't know what to do now, all her friends were gone, and she was scared and all alone. No one can help her, this is her journey, her legacy and at this moment she feels that she has lost. Rain closed her eyes and just hoped she could wish it all away, so that when she opens them everyone will still be there at the festival waiting for her. Rain opened her eyes, rolled on her back, she was soaked in Shelly's blood, and she stared at the ceiling of the building and saw all the levels, then her heart raced because somewhere up there she will find the meaning behind all of this. Rain noticed something, standing on the highest level of the building a faint figure stood staring down at her. Rain got up quickly. "hey!!!" She shouted. The figure moved away from the balcony. "Hey I need help!!" She shouted again. Rain dried her eyes, grabbed Shelly's sword, and ran to the stairs that lead to the top. "Okay, Rain don't be scared you can do this." She told herself as she ran up the stairs, passing by skeletons, old machines, papers, and chairs. The steps had old bloodstained hand prints from people trying to get away from the Junaks, and body parts scattered everywhere. Rain didn't let the horror of what's happened in the past or the present get to her head because it may drive her mad, and at this moment with all that has happened to her she is only seconds from losing her mind. Rain made it to the top floor, she looked around all she saw was one silver door, all the rest of the level was a white wall. "Where are you!!!" Rain shouted but no one answered. "I know you're here!!!" She shouted again. Rain fell to her knees and cried, she felt that maybe she did lose her mind, because not only did she lose her friends, but she feels she has forgotten reality, she was so truly frightened of being alone, and could no longer bear the thought of what was to come next. Her eyes widened as her anxieties began to rush through her and the sickness of seeing her friends die was setting in, she grew more and more dizzy and nauseous and began to heave and gag but held it in and took a deep breath to calm herself down as she wept. Rain put her hand on the rail of the stairs. "Rain pull yourself together, you're going to be okay. Just finish this. go into the room and put an end to all of this. You can do it, yeah, you can do it." She kept telling herself as she fought hard to stay strong. Rain stood up and kept shaking. "I'm fucking scared!!!" She screamed at the top of her lungs trying to wash away her anxiety by drawing to her true feelings. Rain was breathing heavily with tears in her eyes. "You shouldn't be." A voice from behind her said. Rain turned suddenly more scared than she had ever been, and there stood Madame Oakeress with a disappointed look on her face. "Rain, you are not a coward, you have come too far to give up now." Madame Oakeress continued. Rains eyes grew wide as she stood shocked at Madame Oakeress's presence. "Rain, you have the world in your hands right now and if you give up everyone is going to die." Madame Oakeress said. Rain let the moment sink in while she grew with rage. "How did you get here?" Rain asked. "I know a spell that can transfer me wherever I choose, but it only works for the person casting the spell no one else, and I knew I would find you here." Madame Oakeress replied. "You could have done this yourself the whole time!!!" Rain shouted. "Rain calm down." Madame Oakeress said. "No!!!!" Rian yelled as she grabbed a chair from the floor threw it angrily over the rails. "My friends are dead because of you!! Now I must tell their families what happened! Look at me I'm no fucking hero, I'm just some fucking girl who had to do a job for you!! I would have rather died in the village oblivious to the world beyond it!! I'm no hero I couldn't even save my friends and you really think I could save the world? Yeah, fuck, and you know what? You told me not to trust anyone because they might be Kenya, well I have trusted everyone, and now I realize I can't trust you!! You ruined everything!!!" Rain finished shouting and looked away from Madame Oakeress. "Do you really think I don't know this!! I didn't want any of this to happen to you or Jillian or shelly and Olive!! I have known all of you, since you all were born. The four of you were like daughters to me I taught you all everything, and you really think their deaths mean nothing to me!!" Madame Oakeress eyes watered. Rains anger started to calm. "Rain, the spirits within the flame won't let me stop the Junaks because it is not my future…. it is yours. Only you can fulfill your future just like everyone else. I am forbidden to do this task, they will tell me your future, but I am not allowed to tell you what happens, only you can see it through and find out for yourself." Madame Oakeress lowered her head and closed her eyes saddened by the argument. Rain walked up to Madame Oakeress and hugged her tightly hoping she never had to let go. Madame Oakeress hugged her back. "I'm so scared." Rain said as she sobbed. "You are braver than you know." Madame Oakeress replied. "All my friends died because of me. I could have done better." Rain said as she continued to sob. "Rain you did your best, and they died to protect you, just like you would have done for them." Madame Oakeress said in a heartfelt voice. Rain raised her head and let go of Madame Oakeress. "Rain, you need to complete your journey. Through that door lies what you seek." Madame Oakeress told her. Rain stared at the door and thought to herself that her journey is ending although she does not know what is behind that door, she must be ready. "Madame Oakeress, I do not know what will happen just promise that you will wait for me." Rain told her. "I'm here for you, Rain. I promise." Madame Oakeress replied. Rain pulled out her key card and swiped it through the lock. the door slid open and Rain walked in.

The door slammed closed behind her, as the lights came on. The room was completely white, with white ceiling tiles and white floor tiles. The sides of the room had white desks with clear computer monitors on them, with white chairs pushed in. In Center of the room there was one machine that stood no higher than Rains waste. The machine was chrome and had a single button on it. Rain walked up to the machine and was about to press it when a woman's voice came from behind her. "what is your name?" The woman's voice asked. Rain turned quickly and saw a holographic projection of a person in a black long-sleeved dress with long black hair and wearing a white crying mask. "I asked you a question." The woman said. "Rain. Are you Kenya?" Rain asked. "Well I am her mind, so, yes." Kenya said. "How?" Asked Rain. "Kenya built me and gave me all of her knowledge, and memories, she even gave me her body or at least a version of it. Now before you even touch that button, you need to understand something, the Junaks were created for a reason, and that reason being that they were my protectors. People wanted to kill me, although these people were important people, I wanted them to work for me. I wanted them to work under my rule, but they told me no, and I don't like that word very much. I refuse to have someone rule over me for my power is greater and I will conquer who ever stands in my way. I am the ruler of this world no one else. Now before you go accusing me of being an evil dictator or evil queen, you need to understand that this world destroyed its self, religion, war, the fight for equality, governments disagreeing with one another, public violence, corruption and poverty. I simply gave this world the opportunity to die early. Look at me bragging away at my greatness.

How old are you? You look to be in your mid-twenties. Such a pretty young thing, capable of so much, you have no idea. Who sent you here?" Kenya stopped talking and walked up to Rain. "Who sent you?" Kenya asked again politely. "Madame Oakeress." Rain said while scared stiff. "Ah now that is a name I haven't heard in a hundred years maybe even longer, you see Madame Oakeress was my personal assistant, she helped me create everything that is Kenya Corps. When the Junaks broke out that bitch and my son left me here alone. while everyone in Kenya Corps were devoured I locked myself in this room watching the world through camera view be destroyed, you see I have cameras all over this worthless planet, because I own several corporations all over the world that had Junaks placed at each one to protect me wherever I may be. Now that button you were about to press is the only one in existents that can kill my Junaks, it will send off a signal to a satellite, and it will program all the microchips in their heads to release the deadly acid, but I ask you not to do it?" Kenya looked at Rain and tried to touch her hair, but her hand went through her. Rain moved away from her. "Why should I spare them? They have taken everything from me and you want me to let them live?" Rain asked nervous and intimidated by Kenya. "Well I see, you want to be the heroine, the savior. Oh, I bow to you, please forgive me of my sins. No. I think it's time for another question. What do you know about reincarnation?" Kenya asked. "Madame Oakeress taught me everything, she told me you could have become anybody and to not trust anyone." Rain said scared of her daring response. "Me? I never wanted to die, this is my world. I wasn't a big believer in reincarnation my son is living proof of that. Did you meet, my son Michael? You may know him as Zero?" Kenya asked. "Yes, he helped me get here. He died protecting me." Rain said. "He did his job well, I was waiting for you. I was hoping you would come one day, now that you are hear my holographic projection is no longer needed, I'm leaving you with two options, but only choose what your heart tells you. One: You may push the button and save whatever is left of this worthless planet. Or Two: You can do what you were born to do, rule this planet until it is completely extinct." Kenya stayed staring at rain, awaiting her response. "What do you mean by born to do?" Rain asked nervously. Kenya Pulled off her mask, revealing her face and smiled. Rains eyes grew wide as her body shook with fear. It was no reflection, Rain was the reincarnation of Kenya. The projection of Kenya vanished, and Rain was alone again, she thought about everything Kenya said, and how easily Kenya could have tempted her into a dictatorship. Rain pulled out the flower Jillian had given to her and held it tight. Kenya did not realize that Rain had grown up around Madame Oakeress, Jillian, Shelly, and Olive, and that she learned what it means to work together. Rain had some of the best friends she could have ever asked for, and she met Zero who helped Jillian and sacrificed himself for her and Shelly. Rain would have given her life for any them. She set out on this journey with her friends for a reason. She may be the reincarnation of Kenya, but she will never fall to her level as a human being. Rains heart is to pure and her spirit is that of a warrior that fights to save the innocent, not to conquer them, and whatever survivors remain on this planet still have a reason to exist. Rain walked up to the machine closed her eyes and took a deep breath. "Kenya you tried to destroy it. I will save it." She said softly as she pushed the button.

THE
END

Printed in the United States
By Bookmasters